Daniel O'Connell

Liberator

Written by Gaye Shortland
and illustrated by Derry Dillon

Published 2017
Poolbeg Press Ltd

123 Grange Hill, Baldoyle
Dublin 13, Ireland

Text © Poolbeg Press Ltd 2017
A catalogue record for this book is available from the British Library.

ISBN 978 1 78199 857 1

Cover design and illustrations by Derry Dillon
Printed by GPS Colour Graphics Ltd, Alexander Road, Belfast BT6 9HP

IRELAND
ATLANTIC OCEAN
IRISH SEA
DONEGAL
DERRY
ANTRIM
Belfast
TYRONE
Ulster
FERMANAGH
ARMAGH
DOWN
MONAGHAN
SLIGO
LEITRIM
CAVAN
LOUTH
MAYO
ROSCOMMON
LONGFORD
Connacht
WESTMEATH
MEATH
Athlone
Clontarf
DUBLIN
GALWAY
OFFALY
KILDARE
Leinster
LAOIS
WICKLOW
CLARE
Ennis
TIPPERARY
CARLOW
Munster
Doneraile
KILKENNY
WEXFORD
LIMERICK
Tralee
Mallow
KERRY
WATERFORD
Cahersiveen
Cork City
Carhan
Derrynane
CORK

For
Éabha, Séadna & Freya

Hunting Cap

Daniel O'Connell was born at his father's farm at Carhan, on the Atlantic coast of County Kerry, in 1775. Then he was given to another family to rear. This was called 'fostering' and his foster-father was his real father's herdsman. So little Daniel lived happily in a small cottage and spoke only Irish until he was five.

Daniel's uncle, Maurice, was head of the O'Connell family. He was known as 'Hunting Cap' because of the velvet cap he always wore, after the government put a tax on the beaver-felt hats gentlemen wore in those days. Hunting Cap was very rich because he was the smuggling chief of the west coast of Ireland. His big house at Derrynane was near a small bay and could be reached only by sea or horseback as there were no roads there then. This was perfect for smuggling. So things like tea, sugar, brandy and silk were brought in by ship at night, with no tax paid to the government.

Back home with his real family, Daniel learned English, as they spoke both English and Irish. He was taught at home by one of the 'hedge-school' teachers who taught Catholic children secretly, as Catholic schools weren't allowed. This was one of the Penal Laws, made to punish Catholics for rebelling against British rule. For example, no Catholic was allowed to own a gun, vote, buy land, go to university, go to Mass or own a horse worth more than £5.

Soon Hunting Cap, who had no children of his own, decided he would make Daniel his heir. So Daniel spent a lot of time at Derrynane, knowing that one day the house and all its land would be his. And most of Hunting Cap's money.

Revolution!

In 1790, when Daniel was fifteen, Hunting Cap sent him and his brother Maurice to a Catholic school in France. But the French Revolution had begun in 1789 and when the Republic was declared in 1792 things turned very violent. The boys left France just in time! The very same day the French king was beheaded on the guillotine. The boys' carriage was attacked on the way to the boat but they were let go on because they had put rosettes in their hats in the republican colours of red, white and blue. On the boat they met the two Sheares brothers from Cork who boasted that they had seen the King being beheaded and showed them a handkerchief soaked in his blood. Daniel asked why they wanted to see such a horrible thing. "For love of freedom!" they said. But freedom should be won without spilling blood, thought Daniel, and he held to that belief all his life. Five years later the Sheares were hanged, drawn and quartered – a horrible death – for directing the Irish 1798 Rebellion.

After Daniel left France, about 41,000 people were beheaded there, accused of being against the revolution. This was called the Reign of Terror. The boys were lucky to escape with their heads on their shoulders.

A Vow

In 1793 Irish Catholics were allowed to go to university again. Hunting Cap, now Deputy-Governor of Kerry, decided that Daniel should be a barrister, which is a lawyer who pleads in court. Then, just as Daniel was 'called to the Bar', the 1798 rebellion against British rule erupted. It failed and there was terrible slaughter. After that, the British government passed the Act of Union, joining the British and Irish parliaments. Now all decisions about Ireland would be made by the British Parliament in London.

On the 1st January 1801 bells rang out in celebration and Daniel's blood boiled. He vowed to repeal the Union – that is, have it cancelled.

But first he would win Catholic Emancipation, freeing Catholics from all the remaining Penal Laws.

The Counsellor

Daniel quickly became famous as 'The Counsellor'. For him, being a barrister was like performing. Tall and muscular, he was able to project his voice powerfully and move his listeners to laughter or tears like an actor on stage. People attended his cases just for entertainment!

Once, two brothers were accused of setting fire to a police station, using pitch (tar). The witness swore he'd know the smell of pitch anywhere.

"So if there was pitch here in court you'd smell it?" said Daniel.

"Yes."

"But you can't smell pitch now?"

"No."

Then Daniel lifted his own big hat up off the table. Under it was a pot of pitch! "You're a liar!" he cried. "Get down, you rascal!"

The court burst out laughing and the brothers were found 'not guilty'.

Daniel was famous for his insults. So was a market woman who had a stall near the Four Courts. The barristers made bets on who would win a contest. After a long argument Daniel left her gasping. In the end she grabbed a saucepan and tried to hit him. The barristers judged Daniel had won!

Another court case was about whether a dying man had signed his will or his relatives had forged his name. The witness kept repeating that the man had signed "while life was in him". At last Daniel leapt at the truth: "Aha! They put a live fly in his mouth and then placed his hand on the will, didn't they?" He was right! They had done just that so they could swear he signed "while life in him". Everyone was absolutely amazed.

A Love Match

Daniel then fell in love with Mary O'Connell, his 22-year-old cousin. After only a few weeks he decided to marry her.

It went like this:

"Are you engaged, Miss O'Connell?"

"I am not."

"Then will you engage yourself to me?"

"I will."

And that was that.

But there was a problem. Mary had no money – and Hunting Cap wanted Daniel to marry a wealthy heiress from Cork. So they married in secret.

Soon Mary was expecting a baby. Daniel went to confess to Hunting Cap but didn't have the nerve. So he wrote instead. When Hunting Cap got the letter he flew into a rage and disinherited Daniel. Now Daniel would never own Derrynane or get any of Hunting Cap's money.

Mary had a baby boy they called Maurice. In the next fourteen years she had eleven more babies! Sadly, five of them died as many babies did in those times.

Hunting Cap decided to make Daniel's brother John his heir. But then a ship carrying a huge load of brandy sank off the coast – and Hunting Cap got hold of the brandy! Daniel heard that the authorities knew and his uncle might be arrested. So he warned him and soon they were friends again. Now Daniel would inherit Derrynane after all.

Daniel wrote a petition for Catholic Emancipation to Parliament but it was rejected. He didn't give up. His motto was: *Agitate, agitate, agitate!* That is, protest and make trouble! The government then offered him £1200 a year if he promised not to be so violent in his speeches about Emancipation. Daniel said: "I prefer my violence!"

The Duel

In 1815 Daniel fought a duel. He had accused the Dublin Corporation of being "beggarly" and one member, John D'Esterre, took offence. He arrived at the Four Courts brandishing a whip and said he was there to horse-whip Daniel, but when Daniel came out he had disappeared.

D'Esterre was a famous duellist so Daniel expected to be challenged. He chose another famous duellist called McNamara as his 'second' – that is, his assistant. McNamara's nickname was 'Fire-ball'!

D'Esterre's 'second' issued the challenge and Fire-ball said they would meet at a park in Kildare.

Daniel arrived with Fire-ball, a surgeon and a priest. There was a big crowd waiting.

Fire-ball and the other second measured out the distance between the duellists and told them to fire.

D'Esterre fired and the bullet entered the ground at Daniel's feet.

Then it was Daniel's turn. He aimed low and took his shot.

D'Esterre spun and fell. There was a loud roar from the crowd. The surgeon rushed to D'Esterre. The bullet had gone into his stomach. He was bleeding badly.

He died two days later, forgiving Daniel with his last breath. Daniel was shattered as he never meant to kill him. After that, he gave money every year to D'Esterre's family until he died and always wore a black glove on his right hand whenever he received Holy Communion, to show his repentance.

Hunting Hares

All day every day Daniel worked for Emancipation. He rose at five in the morning, spent the day in court and then went on to public meetings. Mary even had to beg him to take a few minutes at lunchtime to eat a bowl of soup.

In 1823 he formed the Catholic Association. Each member paid one penny a month. This money, called the "Catholic Rent", was used to hire lawyers to defend Catholics who broke the Penal Laws, and much more.

Hunting Cap died at the age of 97. Derrynane was now Daniel's. He had bought an expensive house for the family in Dublin, in Merrion Square, but they went to Derrynane often. He loved to walk along the beach alone, in his dressing gown and cap, practising his speeches. Other days, he would set out on foot with his huntsmen and beagles to hunt hares in the mountains. Servants followed them with baskets packed with a big picnic. In the evenings there would be visitors of all nationalities and over thirty people would sit down to dinner together. It was a wonderful life.

Liberation!

At that time men who owned or rented land that was worth forty shillings or more were allowed to vote in elections. This included Catholics who now had been given the right to vote. So Daniel decided to get elected as a member of parliament for County Clare. But he knew that he couldn't take his seat in parliament if he won, because first he'd have to take an oath rejecting the Catholic Church.

He won with a huge number of votes and was carried shoulder-high for hours around the streets of Ennis. Then the British government, seeing how much support he had, granted Catholic Emancipation on the 13th April 1829. This had been Daniel's plan all along.

"*I tread on air!*" he wrote to Mary.

Catholic members of parliament were now allowed to take a new oath that didn't deny the Catholic Church. But the King insisted that Daniel take the old oath because he had been elected before Emancipation. He was jealous of Daniel, calling him the real "King of Ireland".

Daniel refused to take the oath.

Then there was only one thing to do: get elected again!

Green had become the special colour of Liberation and as he drove to Clare again people waved green handkerchiefs or leafy branches at him. One old woman even grabbed a big bunch of nettles and ran along waving them, crying, "Long life to the Liberator!"

He was easily elected. Now he could take his place in parliament.

Celebrity

Daniel by now was a huge celebrity world-wide. The King of Bavaria sent for his autograph. So did the Tsar of Russia but Daniel refused, saying he was a tyrant. But, also, Daniel was a 'folk hero' – a hero of the common people – with people telling stories about him at their firesides at night. They even *made up* stories showing his cleverness and how he was always the winner.

In one story he was in England at an inn when his enemies poisoned his wine. But there was an Irish serving girl there and she spoke to him in Irish so no-one would understand.

"Daniel O'Connell, do you understand Irish?"

"I understand it well, girl from Ireland."

"There's enough poison in your cup to kill hundreds!"

"If that is true, my girl, I'll pay for your dowry."

So, with a wink, Daniel got rid of the poisoned wine!

Night ride

In 1829, twenty-two men from Doneraile, County Cork, were accused of planning to murder some important Protestants. The trial was in Cork City and on the first day, a Friday, four men were condemned to be hanged. Then William Burke, the brother of one of the prisoners, mounted the best horse in Cork and rode 90 miles through the night to Derrynane.

Daniel agreed to take the case. William rode back to Cork. "O'Connell's coming, boys!" he yelled.

Daniel drove in a fast light carriage through Sunday night and the Solicitor-General was already addressing the jury when he walked into court on Monday morning. As he'd had no breakfast, he asked if he could have a bowl of milk and some sandwiches brought in to him. The judge allowed this.

The Solicitor-General continued. Daniel, with his mouth full of bread and milk, kept interrupting him: "That's not law!" and "That's no longer law!" and so on.

Then Daniel cleverly cross-examined the witnesses.

In the end the men were freed, and the four men already sentenced to hang were transported to Australia instead – one of the punishments of the time.

Lord Mayor

In 1836 Mary fell ill. "God help me!" cried Daniel when she died. He could never speak of her without crying for the rest of his life.

He refused another important job offered by the British government and instead fought on for Repeal as he knew Mary would want him to do that. He formed the Repeal Association and young, energetic figures joined it. He called them the 'Young Irelanders'.

In 1841 he was elected Lord Mayor of Dublin for one year. Speaking from the corporation balcony in his crimson robe of office and cocked hat, he had fun with the people, asking: "Does the hat suit me?" and "How about the gold chain?"

He was an excellent mayor and very fair to all.

Monster Meetings

In 1843 Daniel held meetings all over the country, called 'Monster Meetings' because of the enormous numbers of people who attended them. The government became very nervous.

In Mallow there were up to 400, 000 people with twenty-six bands playing and the army was called out. But the crowd kept the peace and the army had no excuse to touch them.

Afterwards, about 600 men attended a dinner in a hall and the gallery was full of women. Daniel had often said that the Irish were like slaves to the British. Now he asked a singer for a song which said: *'Oh, where's the slave so lowly, Condemn'd to chains unholy . . .'*

On hearing those words Daniel jumped to his feet and threw out his arms.

"I AM NOT THAT SLAVE!" he shouted.

"WE ARE NOT THOSE SLAVES!" roared all the people, leaping up too.

At Athlone Daniel told the crowd that it was big enough to throw all its enemies into the River Shannon but that "By keeping on a peaceful path the day of our freedom will draw near!" After his speech he sat down like a boxer after a bout, a big cloak around his shoulders. A man handed him a peach and he took a big bite. Then he signed the albums of lady admirers.

At another meeting he was presented with a green velvet cap shaped like an ancient Irish crown. He called this 'The Repeal Cap' and promised to wear it for the rest of his life. And he did.

All was going wonderfully well but at Clontarf, where the High King Brian Boru won a great battle in 1014, the government banned the meeting. A large army with heavy artillery moved into position, as did three gunships out at sea.

Daniel had a huge decision to make. Then he cancelled the meeting because it would have ended in slaughter.

The Young Irelanders were not happy. They felt he had backed down.

Arrest

In 1843 Daniel, with six others, was arrested on a number of false charges. The jury was selected but then any Catholics in it were dismissed which was a terrible injustice.

Daniel was sentenced to twelve months' imprisonment in Richmond prison, Dublin, and the others to nine months. But they had such a good time there it became known as 'The Richmond Picnic'! They rented rooms in the house of the governor, and their families came to live with them. Daniel even had his young grandson Daniel with him. The prison had gardens and an artist's studio to paint their portraits and make daguerreotypes, an early kind of photograph. From the first day presents started to arrive: meat, fish, fruit and even a gigantic cake. And seven musical boxes! And they had lots of visitors. Daniel said they were all "cheerful as larks".

Then an appeal was made and the Lord Chief Justice in London said that if Daniel's sentence was allowed to stand "trial by jury in Ireland would become a mockery". So Daniel's sentence was overturned.

The news was carried to Ireland by ship. On the quay a banner was unfurled: 'O'CONNELL IS FREE!' and thousands of men, women and children rushed there with white flags. The banner was then put on the engine of a train which carried the news around the country.

Two messengers raced to take the news to Daniel. The younger one raced ahead, shouting *"I'm first! I'm first!"* He threw open the door to the room where Daniel was sitting. *"You're free, Liberator, you're free!"*

The next day a 'triumphal chariot', drawn by six white horses, arrived at the prison door. It was covered in purple velvet and gold fringe and it had three levels. On the lowest level sat Daniel's grandchildren dressed in green velvet tunics and caps with white feathers. On the middle one sat an old harper, dressed as an ancient Irish bard. On top sat Daniel on a chair, wearing his green velvet cap, with his chaplain.

They set out through huge cheering crowds.

There were hundreds of bonfires lit all over the country that night.

Slavery

But some of the Young Irelanders didn't agree with Daniel's ideas. They believed that liberty was "worth some blood-letting". And they wanted an Irish Republic, not just Repeal of the Union.

And they didn't all agree with him on slavery. Daniel hated slavery passionately. In 1833 the British had forbidden slavery in their colonies – but there was still slavery in America. Daniel wrote a letter to the Irish people in America, signed by 60,000 Irish people, begging them to oppose slavery. But many Irish-Americans who were sending money to him to support

Repeal thought slavery was a good thing. The Young Irelanders begged Daniel to stop agitating about slavery but he refused. If that meant no more money from America, then so be it.

With these splits the Repeal movement was not as strong as before.

The Great Famine

Then tragedy struck. Daniel's beloved grandson, little Daniel, died in 1844 and this crushed him. And in 1845 the potatoes growing in the ground began to rot, because of a disease called 'blight'. And potatoes were the main food of the poor people. Ireland was bursting with food of all kinds but the poor couldn't afford to buy any of it. Instead they ate potatoes in their skins three times a day.

Daniel begged the government to provide food and work, otherwise thousands of people would starve and diseases like typhus would kill thousands more. He was right. In the next few years one million people starved to death or died from disease. And one million had to leave Ireland for ever to escape starvation, in what were known as 'coffin ships' as so many people died in them.

The government ignored Daniel. So he did what he could, buying 10 tons of Indian meal and 10 tons of oatmeal and sending them to Kerry.

He became sick from all the stress but, even so, he travelled to London. There, in parliament, he pleaded: "Ireland is in your hands – she cannot save herself!"

But the government took no action and every day, under armed guard, ships laden with food of all sorts left Ireland to be sold in England while families starved and fell by the wayside.

End of the Struggle

Broken-hearted, Daniel set out to travel to Rome to see the Pope. He knew he was about to die. He reached Genoa in Italy but there collapsed. An Italian doctor applied leeches to suck his blood, which they believed was a cure, but of course it did no good.

Then, his hands clasped in prayer, Daniel died.

When the doctors did an autopsy they found his brain was horribly enflamed. This had killed him. His great heart, now still for ever, was sent to Rome in a silver urn.

His body was taken back to Ireland by sea in a steamer. The news had gone ahead and when the people of Dublin saw the plume of smoke on the horizon, rich and poor rushed down to the docks.

A 'coffin ship' crowded with starving people was making its way out to sea on its journey to America. Many of them would be dead before they reached the end of the voyage. When their ship passed the steamer from Italy their terrible wails of grief rose to the sky, as they knew the man who had tried so hard to save them was gone forever.

The steamer reached the dock. On the deck was a 'sea chapel' which was a tent draped in black velvet, with gold embroidery and silver tassels. When the curtains were drawn and the thousands of people saw the coffin inside they all fell to their knees and wept. On the coffin was a silver plaque saying:

Daniel O'Connell, Ireland's Liberator.

He was buried in Glasnevin and a round tower was built over his grave to mark it. His statue overlooks O'Connell Street in Dublin, the street named after him.

We must hope he would be as proud of us today as we are proud of him.

The End

GLOSSARY (alphabetical order)

agitate: to protest; or to disturb something

appeal: a request to a court to reverse a legal decision

artillery: large field guns

association: a group joined together for a special purpose

audacious: disrespectful

autopsy: examination of a body to discover the cause of death

ban: to officially stop something

bard: traditional poet who spoke or sang his poetry

beaver-felt: material made of beaver fur

beggarly: mean

bout: a short period of activity

called to the Bar: become a barrister

campaign: a planned course of action to achieve some aim

celebrity: famous person

charges: accusations, especially by the law

chaplain: a priest attached to a private chapel (like in a big house)

corporation: a group of people elected to govern a city or town

counsellor: a person trained to give advice; or a barrister

deputy: someone who takes charge when a superior is absent

drape: arrange cloth or clothes loosely over or around something

drawn: disembowelled, meaning to 'have their intestines pulled out'

election: choosing people by voting

emancipation: the freeing of someone (from slavery, for instance)

enflamed: reddened, swollen from infection or injury

erupt: break out suddenly

folk: people in general

grief: sorrow

guillotine: machine for beheading people

40

hedge-school: secret country school for Catholic children

heir (male)/heiress (female): person who inherits from a person who has died

herdsman: person taking care of a herd of animals

jury: group who decide in court if a person is guilty

leech: a bloodsucking worm

Liberator: a person who frees others

lowly: low in importance

mayor: head of a town elected by the town council

meal: the edible part of any grain ground to powder

oath: a solemn promise

parliament: group of people elected to govern a country

plaque: a flat piece of metal with writing in memory of someone or some event

plume: a feather; or a long cloud of smoke rising upward

portrait: a painting of a person

project: to throw or direct something forwards, with force

pugnacious: eager to fight

reign: period of rule

repeal: the taking back of a law, cancelling it

repentance: state of being sorry

republic: country where the power is held by the people and their representatives

revolution: overthrow of a government

slaughter: killing in a bloody manner

stress: strain or tension

tread: walk, step

triumphal: made or used in celebration of victory

tyrant: a cruel ruler

urn: a tall vase, especially one for storing ashes of a cremated person

vow: promise solemnly

wail: high-pitched cry of grief or pain

wept: cried

Some Things to Talk About

1.   Where did Daniel live when he was a baby?

2.   Why was Daniel's uncle called 'Hunting Cap'?

3.   How did Hunting Cap become rich?

4.   Where did Daniel go to school?

5.   What were the Penal Laws?

6.   What happened the day Daniel and his brother left France?

7.   Who were the Sheares brothers?

8.   Did Daniel believe in violent rebellion?

9.   What was the Act of Union?

10. What did 'Catholic Emancipation' mean?

11. What trick did Daniel play in court to catch out a lying witness?

12. What did Hunting Cap do when Daniel got married? Why?

13. Why did the government offer Daniel £1200 a year?

14. Tell the story of the duel Daniel fought.

15. Why did Daniel love Derrynane so much, do you think?

16. Why couldn't Daniel take his seat in parliament?

17. What did 'Repeal' mean?

18. What was the 'Catholic Rent'?

19. What is a 'folk hero'?

20. What kind of stories did the people like to tell about Daniel?

21. Why did Daniel go to the court in Cork to defend some prisoners?

22. What were the 'Monster Meetings'? Why did Daniel hold them?

23. Why did Daniel believe peaceful means would win Repeal?

24. What happened at the Clontarf meeting?

25. Who were the Young Irelanders?

26. What was called 'The Richmond Picnic'?

27. How did Daniel feel about slavery?

28. What happened when the potatoes got a disease in Ireland?

29. Why were the 'coffin ships' given that name?

30. Many believe Daniel was the greatest Irishman ever. Do you agree?

31. Why was Daniel so loved by the people of Ireland, do you think?

Timeline

1775: Daniel O'Connell is born on 6th August
1789: French Revolution begins
1792: French Republic is declared
1798: Daniel becomes a barrister
United Irishmen rebellion in Ireland fails
1800: Act of Union is passed in Britain
1801: Act of Union comes into effect on 1st January
1803: Robert Emmet's rebellion in Ireland fails
1811: King George III goes insane; his son George takes over
1817: First Total Abstinence Society in Europe founded in County Cork
1820: Death of George III; George IV crowned
1823: Daniel founds the Catholic Association
1828: Daniel is elected MP for County Clare
1829: Catholic Emancipation is granted
Daniel is re-elected, takes seat in parliament
1830: Opening of Dublin Zoo, second oldest in the world
Death of George IV; William IV crowned
1836: Mary O'Connell dies
1837: Death of William IV; Queen Victoria crowned
1838: Father Mathew's temperance movement founded
1840: Repeal Association founded by Daniel
1841: Daniel becomes Lord Mayor of Dublin for one-year term
1843: Monster Meetings held in many locations
Clontarf Monster Meeting cancelled by Daniel
1844: Daniel gaoled in Richmond prison
1845: Beginning of potato blight
1846: Famine
Young Irelanders withdraw from Repeal Association
1847: Famine continues
Daniel dies in Genoa on 15th May